Animals should definitely <u>not</u> wear clothing.

Written by Judi Barrett and drawn by Ron Barrett

SCHOLASTIC INC.
New York Toronto London Auckland Sydney

For Amy and Valerie

ISBN 0-590-44739-4

Copyright © 1970 by Judi Barrett.
Drawings copyright © 1970 by Ron Barrett.
All rights reserved. Published by Scholastic Inc., 730 Broadway, New York, NY 10003, by arrangement with Aladdin Books, a division of Macmillan Publishing Co.

12 11 10 9 8 7   1 2 3 4 5 6/9

Printed in the U.S.A.   08

First Scholastic printing, February 1991

Animals should definitely _not_ wear clothing...

because
it would be
disastrous for
a porcupine,

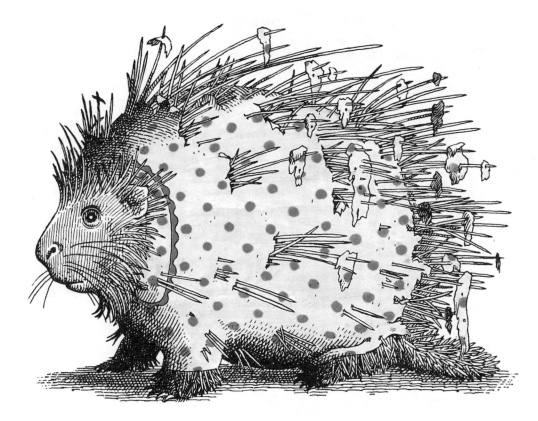

because
a camel
might wear it
in the wrong
places,

because
a snake would
lose it,

because

a mouse

could get lost

in it,

because
a sheep
might find it
terribly hot,

because
it could be
very messy
for a pig,

because
it might
make life hard
for a hen,

because
a kangaroo
would find it
quite
unnecessary,

because
a giraffe
might look
sort of silly,

because
a billy goat
would eat it
for lunch,

because
it would always
be wet
on a walrus,

because
a moose
could never
manage,

because
opossums
might wear it
upside down
by mistake,

and most of all,
because
it might be
very
embarrassing.